PET STORIES
You Don't Have to Walk

SeaStar Books

NEW YORK

Special thanks to Leigh Ann Jones, Valerie Lewis, Walter Mayes, and Marian Reiner for the consultation services and invaluable support they provided for the creation of this book.

Reading Rainbow® is a production of GPN/Nebraska ETV and WNED-TV Buffalo and is produced by Lancit Media Entertainment, Ltd., a JuniorNet Company. *Reading Rainbow®* is a registered trademark of GPN/WNED-TV.

 SeaStar Books · A division of North-South Books, Inc.

ISBN 1-58717-032-9 (library binding) 10 9 8 7 6 5 4 3 2 1
ISBN 1-58717-031-0 (paperback) 10 9 8 7 6 5 4 3 2 1

Contents

The Best Pet

BY Laurie Krasny Brown

PICTURES BY Marc Brown

"Now that you do your own jobs,
you can have your own pets!" said Dad.
"Let's get them now!" said Rex and Lilly.

"Dad, may I have a dog?" asked Rex.

"A dog is the best pet!"

"No, Rex, not a dog," said Dad.

"A dog is too much trouble."

"Dad, may I have a cat?" asked Lilly.

"A cat is the best pet."
"No, Lilly, not a cat," said Dad.
"A cat is too much trouble."

"How about a bird?" asked Lilly.
"A bird can be the best pet!"

"No, not a bird either," said Dad.

"Too much trouble."

"No dog! No cat!" said Rex.

"Then what pet *can* we have?"

"Fish!" said Dad. "Fish are the best pets. And they are not too much trouble."

"I like the yellow fish," said Lilly.

"I like the blue fish," said Rex.

Lilly put her fish in the tank.
Rex put his fish in, too.
The fish swam and swam.
"Is that all they do?" asked Rex.

A week later, Lilly said, "Look, Rex!
Look at all the fish!"
"Wow!" said Rex.

"Fish *are* the best pets!" said Rex.

"And we get more all the time!" said Lilly.

Why Not Get a Pterodactyl

BY Lee Bennett Hopkins

PICTURE BY Henry Cole

Why not get
a pterodactyl
for a pet—

to strap me high
upon its wings
and fly into
an unknown sky—

with every eye
to watch my flight
as I clutch
my pterodactyl tight

and disappear
into the night?

A Dog's Tale

BY Seymour Reit

PICTURES BY Kate Flanagan

When I was a tiny puppy,
I lived at the pound.
But I was very lonely.
I wanted a person to love–
a person all my own.

Then, one wonderful day,
I saw Wendy.
She was just right for me!
So I let her take me home.

Wendy was a good kid,
but she never had a puppy before.
She had lots to learn.
Lucky she had me to teach her!

First I helped her pick my name.
She called me Spot, then Skippy.
When she called me Ruff,
I barked, "Ruff! Ruff! Ruff!"

I had to teach her that puppies
eat at least three times a day.
I always remind her
if she forgets!

I even had to teach Wendy
that puppies need
lots of fresh water.

Wendy finally got the hang of it.
She found a big box and
made a warm, cozy bed for me.

But sometimes I just have to snuggle in Wendy's bed. It makes her so happy!

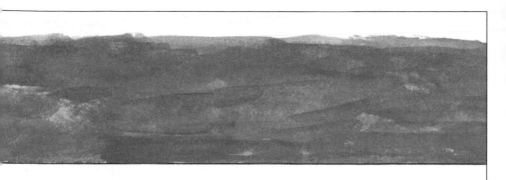

The Kittens

BY Cynthia Rylant

PICTURES BY Suçie Stevenson

In May the cat who lived
next door to Henry and Mudge
had a litter of kittens.
There were five kittens.
One was orange.
One was gray.
One was black and white.
And two were all black.

The kittens sometimes stayed
in a box in their front yard
to get some sun
while the mother cat rested.
One day Henry and Mudge
peeked in the box.
They saw tiny little
kitten faces
and tiny little
kitten paws
and heard tiny little
kitten meows.

Mudge sniffed
and sniffed and sniffed.
He wagged his tail
and sneezed
and sniffed some more.
Then he put his
big head into the box,
and with his big tongue
he licked
all five kittens.

Henry laughed.
"So you want
some kittens of your own?"
he asked Mudge.
Mudge grunted
and wagged his tail again.
Whenever the kittens
were in their front yard,
Henry and Mudge
visited the box.
Henry loved their
little noses.
And he had even
given them names.

He called them
Venus,
Earth,
Mars,
Jupiter,
and Saturn.
Henry loved planets, too.

While Henry was at school one day,
a new dog came up Henry's street.
The five kittens
were sleeping
in the box in their yard.
Mudge was sleeping in Henry's house.

When the new dog
got closer to Henry's house,
Mudge's ears went up.

When the new dog
got even closer
to Henry's house,
Mudge's nose went in the air.
And just when the new dog
was in front of
Henry's house,
Mudge barked.

He barked and barked
and barked
until Henry's mother
opened the door.

And just as
Mudge ran out the door,
the new dog
was in the neighbor's yard,
looking in the kittens' box.
And just as the new dog
was putting his big teeth
into the box,
Mudge ran up behind him.

SNAP! went Mudge's teeth
when the new dog saw him.
SNAP! went Mudge's teeth again
when the new dog looked back
at the box of kittens.

Mudge growled.

He looked into the eyes of the new dog.

He stood ready to jump.

And the new dog backed away
from the box.

He didn't want the kittens anymore.

He just wanted to leave.

And he did.

Mudge looked in the kitten box.
He saw five tiny faces
and five skinny tails
and twenty little paws.
He reached in and licked
all five kittens.

Then he lay down
beside the box
and waited for Henry.
Venus,
Earth,
Mars,
Jupiter,
and Saturn
went back to sleep.

My Fish Can Ride a Bicycle

BY Jack Prelutsky • PICTURE BY James Stevenson

My fish can ride a bicycle,
my fish can climb a tree,
my fish enjoys a glass of milk,
my fish takes naps with me.

My fish can play the clarinet,
my fish can bounce a ball,
my fish is not like other fish,
my fish can't swim at all.

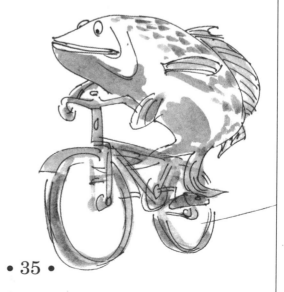

SELECTIONS FROM

Danny and the Dinosaur

BY Syd Hoff

Danny loved dinosaurs.
He wished he had one.
"I'm sorry they are not
real," said Danny.
"It would be nice to
play with a dinosaur."

"And I think it would be
nice to play with you,"
said a voice.
"Oh, good," said Danny.
"What can we do?"

"I can take you
for a ride,"
said the dinosaur.
He put his head down
so Danny could
get on him.

"Let's go!" said Danny.

A policeman stared at them.
He had never seen
a dinosaur stop
for a red light.

The dinosaur was so tall
Danny had to hold up
the ropes for him.

"Look out!" said Danny.

"Bow wow!" said a dog,
running after them.
"He thinks you are a car,"
said Danny. "Go away, dog.
We are not a car."

"I can make a noise
like a car,"
said the dinosaur.
"Honk! Honk! Honk!"

"I love to climb,"
said the dinosaur.
"Down, boy!" said Danny.

Some people were
waiting for a bus.
They rode on the
dinosaur's tail instead.

"All who want to
cross the street,
may walk on my back,"
said the dinosaur.

Danny and the dinosaur
went all over town and
had lots of fun.
"It's good to take an
hour or two off after a
hundred million years,"
said the dinosaur.

The Good Day

BY Sara Swan Miller

PICTURES BY True Kelley

One day your friend went to the door.
"I am going out, Kitty," said your friend.
"Now be good. Don't do anything bad
while I am gone."
Your friend went out the door.

"Why would I want to do anything bad?"
you asked yourself. "Bad things are no good."
Your friend was so silly!

You looked around for
something good to do.
A curtain was blowing
in the wind.
"Climbing is always fun,"
you said to yourself.
"And fun is good!"
You stuck out your strong
claws. You began to climb
up the curtain. You climbed
all the way to the top.

Then you jumped
back down.

"That was a very good thing
to do," you said to yourself.
"I think I will do it again."

So you climbed up the curtain again.
Then you climbed it again.

And again.

And again.

"Hm," you said to yourself. "There
are too many holes in this curtain now.
But it was very good while it lasted!"

You looked around for something else good
to do. A green plant was growing on the
windowsill. You jumped up next to it.
"This plant looks good," you said.
You nibbled on a leaf. The plant was VERY
good. You nibbled all the nice green tips.

"Mmmmm," you said to yourself.
"That was very, very good."

A little rug was lying on the floor.
"Cleaning my claws is always a good thing
to do," you said to the rug.
You sunk your claws into the rug.
You worked and worked. You worked until
your claws were good and clean and sharp.

"Ah," you said to yourself.
"That was very, very, very good."

A bowl was sitting on the table. You jumped up next to it. You looked in the bowl. There was something inside! You stuck your paw in the bowl and felt all around.

"What is this Thing in the bowl?" you asked yourself. "It would be good to find out."

You fished around in the bowl.
The Thing would not come out!

You fished around some more.
And some more.

CRASH!

The bowl fell on the floor.

You jumped down and looked at the Thing.

You gave it a poke.

"Oh," you said to the Thing.

"You are just a piece of paper.

Oh well. It is good to know, anyway."

You went looking for more good things to do.
You prowled all around the house.
You prowled here.

You prowled there.

Finally, you prowled your way into the
kitchen. A can was sitting on the floor.
"What is that Good Smell?" you asked the
can. "It would be very, very good to find out."

You knocked off the lid and looked inside.
You stuck in your paw. Was this the Good
Smell? No. You tossed it on the floor.
Was this the Good Smell? No. Or this?
No. Or this? You dug and dug in the can.
You dug all the way to the bottom.

"Aha!" you said. "Here you are, Smell!"
A wonderful piece of chicken!
"This is better than good," you said.
"This is GREAT!"

You munched and you crunched.
You crunched and you munched.
You munched and crunched up every last bit.

"Mmmmm," you said. "Ahhh!
That was the best thing I have done all day!"

Doing all those good things
made you very sleepy.
You crept back to the living room.
You jumped up on the couch
and curled yourself into a ball.
"What a good day I had today!"
you said to yourself.

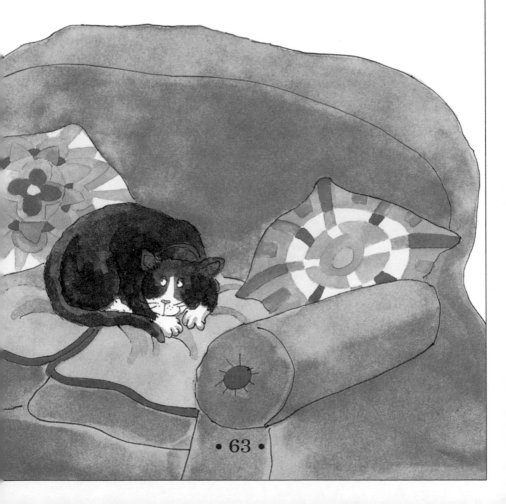

"My friend will be happy.
I did not do one bad thing!"
You wrapped your tail over your nose,
and you went to sleep.

The End